APR 1 7 2008

D0515511

FiSHy
FrieNdS

Michael Patrick O'Neill

RETA E KING LIBRARY
CHADRON STATE COLLEGE
CHADRON, NE 69337

Copyright©Michael Patrick O'Neill
All Rights Reserved.

The photographs in this book have not been
enhanced digitally and are protected by
national and international copyright laws.
No part of this book may be reproduced
without the written permission
of the publisher.

O'Neill, Michael Patrick
Fishy Friends / Michael Patrick O'Neill
ISBN 0-9728653-0-6
LCCN 2003090555

Cover, Graphics & Illustration: George Milek
Printed in China

Batfish Books
PO Box 32909
Palm Beach Gardens, FL 33420-2909
E-mail: info@batfishbooks.com
www.batfishbooks.com
Author's Website
www.mpostock.com

10 9 8 7 6 5 4 3 2 1

591.77
On 2f

Dedicated to Joseph W. O'Neill

(1926–2002)

Thanks for leaving the best footprints to be followed.

Welcome
to our Fascinating,
undersea World.

My name's Charlie the Crab, and I'm going to take you on an incredible journey through the briny depths, where you'll meet a bunch of my wonderfully wacky and weird pals and learn about our home, the world's oceans.

Put on your mask and get ready. A voyage of adventure awaits you!

The Earth's Oceans are a Treasure Chest, Filled With an Infinite Number of Jewels.

Each one with a different sparkle.

Each one with a different story to tell.

All of them fascinating.

All of them woven together in a magical web of life.

Let's get happily lost.
Let's go where the fish go.
Let's dive in and learn about these mesmerizing jewels.

FiNderS KeeperS!

It'S Said that oNe maN'S trash iS aNother'S treaSure.

I'm a Seaweed Blenny and couldn't agree more!

From my home in this old bottle, I can hide and watch the world swim by.

Isn't it amazing that nothing goes to waste on the bottom of the sea?

I'M a CoNe SHeLL HerMit Crab, aND LiKe tHe SeaWeeD BLeNNY, I'M aLWaYS oN tHe LooKout For a rooF over My HeaD.

Instead of old bottles, I prefer empty shells that look like ice cream cones; hence, their name — cone shells!

These shells are perfect, since I can squeeze my thin body inside and keep my colorful legs outside, allowing me to crawl around the bottom.

When I get too big for my home, I simply find a bigger shell and switch.

I have to lose some weight before I can squeeze into that thing!

Talking about that little guy with the colorful legs, I also have a shell as a home, but that's where the similarity ends.

You see, I'm a Queen Conch and my shell is part of my body. As I get bigger, it also gets bigger.

It's very tough and heavy and offers awesome protection, leaving only my eyes and whiskers out in the open so I can see where I'm going.

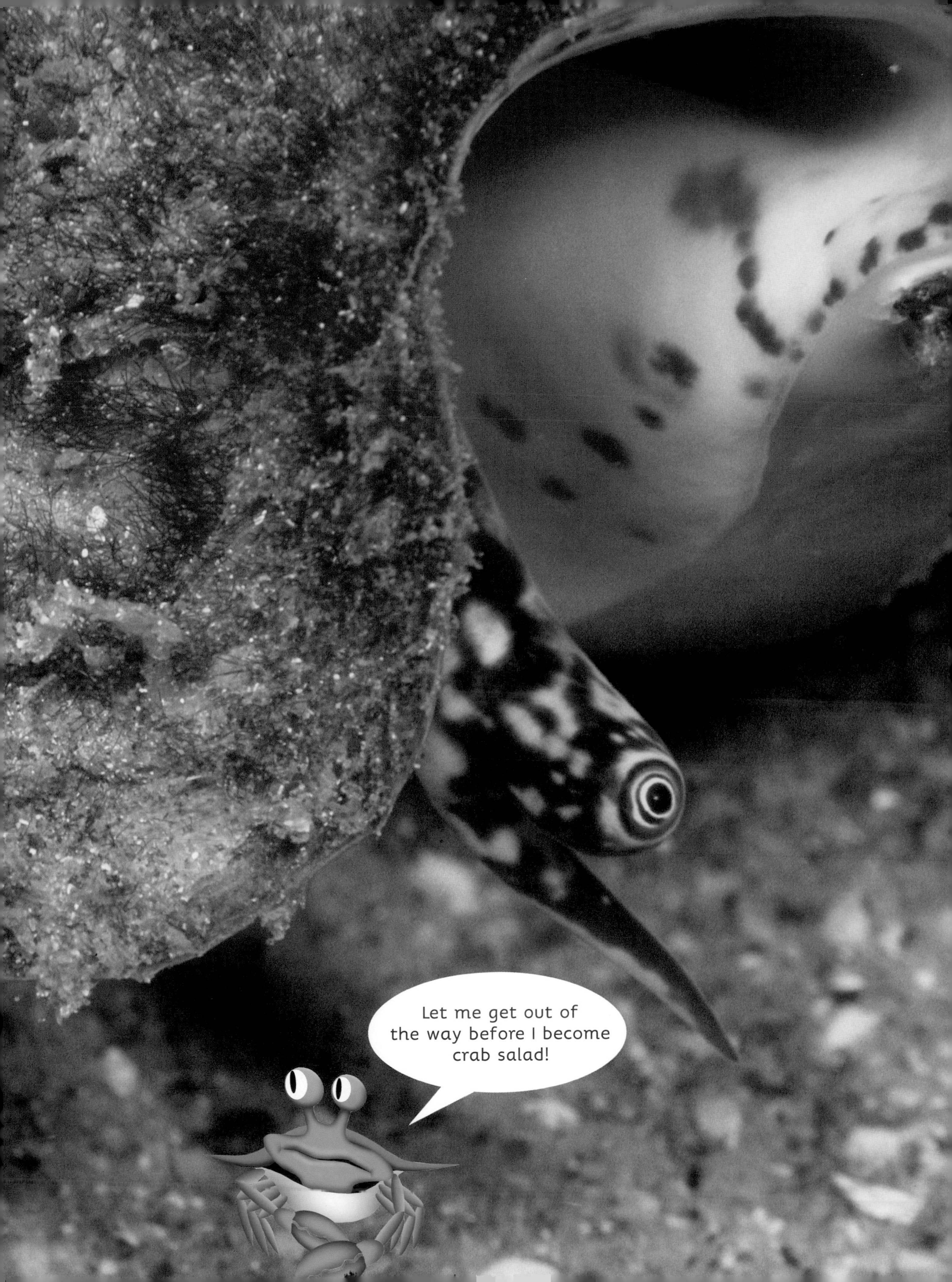
Let me get out of the way before I become crab salad!

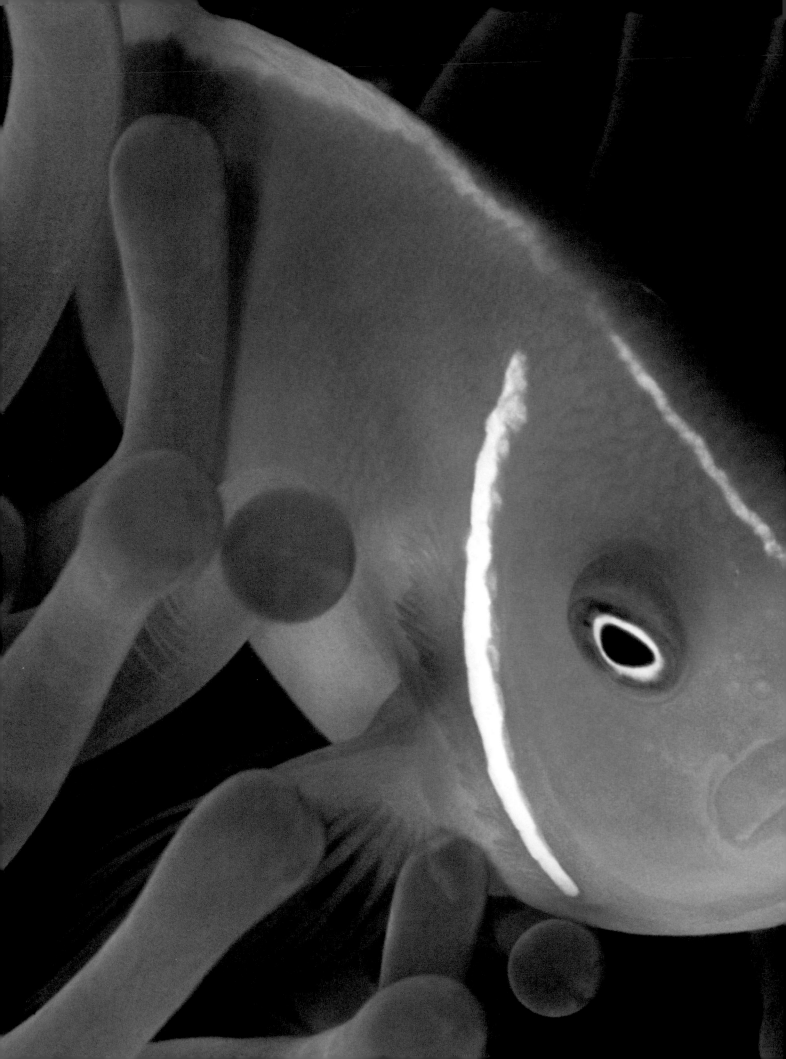

IF you thiNK ONLy OLD bottLes aND SHeLLs MaKe gooD HOMeS ON the oceaN bottoM, thiNK aGaiN!

A Clownfish like me can only be found in a Sea Anemone.

Why are you called a Clownfish and what's a Sea Anemone?

The neighbors call me Clownfish because I clown around! And this bunch of colorful, gooey "spaghetti" is a Sea Anemone, and she protects me. You'll never see me far away from her, the reason why I'm also called an Anemonefish.

Her arms sting other fish, but I have a special trick — an invisible shield — that lets me move through her tentacles without getting hurt. It's like sitting on a beehive and not getting stung.

At night, she covers me like a big, shaggy blanket.

TaLK abouT getting tucKeD iN.

RETA E. KING LIBRARY
CHADRON STATE COLLEGE
CHADRON, NE 69337

WHat in the World?

Okay. Okay. I can explain everything. Promise.

I'm what's called a Decorator Crab. Can you guess why?

Where I live, it seems everybody craves juicy and tasty crab legs! Can you believe it?

WHat Nerve!

So, to hide myself, I go to a secret garden where tiny, Strawberry Anemones grow. There, I pick out a few little "buttons" and plant them on my back. And with this crazy costume, I cover up pretty well.

How about a game of Hide & Seek? Can you find the Decorator Crab below?

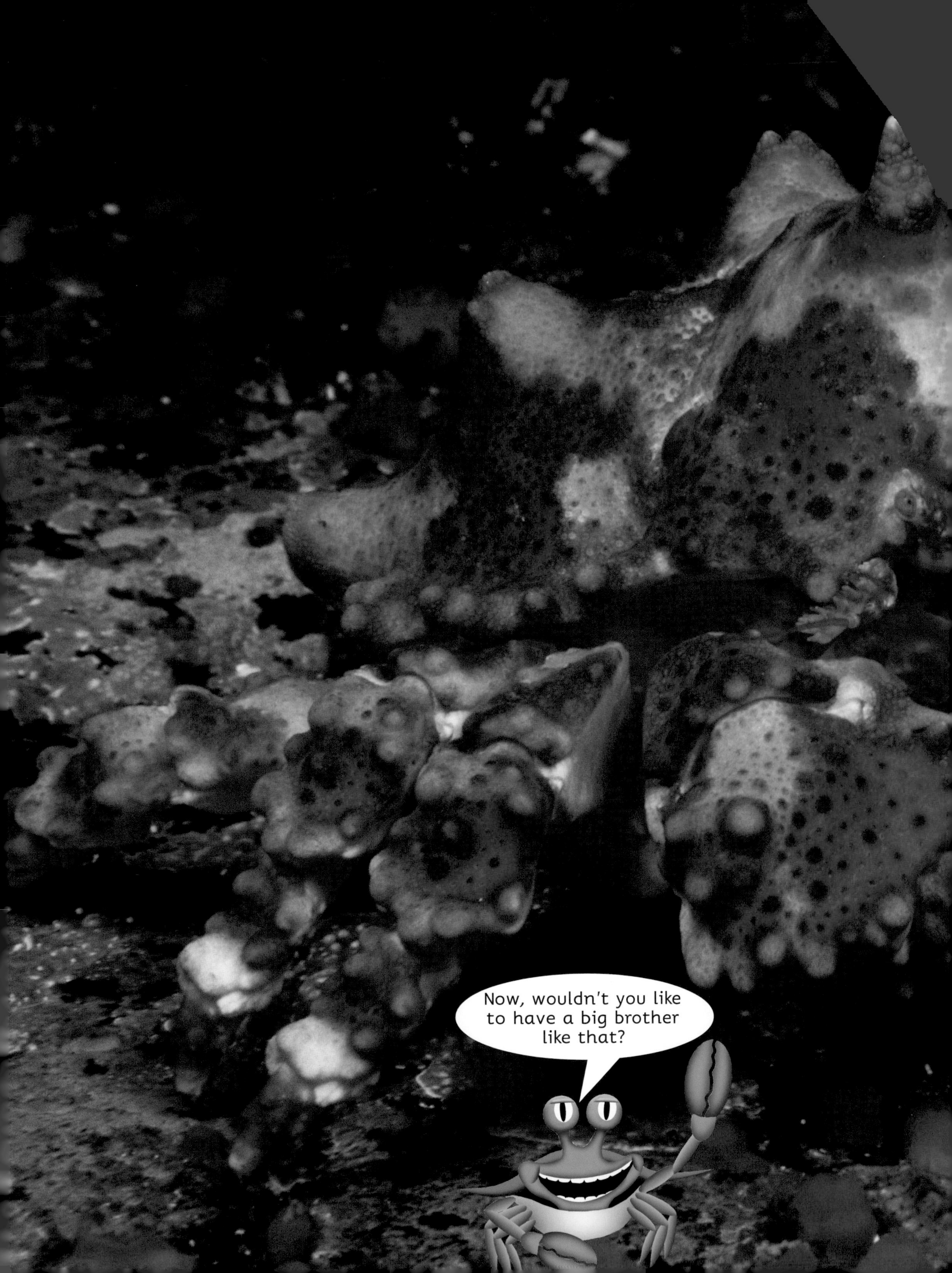
Now, wouldn't you like
to have a big brother
like that?

Space Invader? A Monster From the Movies?

Nope! Boys and girls, I'm the Real Deal.

I'm a Puget Sound King Crab, and if the Decorator Crab is the King of Costumes, then I'm King of the Hill.

Think of me as a monster truck, the all-wheel-drive of the underwater world. With my strong shell, horns and beefy legs, I go wherever I please, so lookout!

Stick or Fish?
One or the other?
Or Both?

I'll admit it — a little of both if you can believe it.

I'm a Stick Pipefish, a shy little fish that avoids the rumble and tumble the Puget Sound King Crab loves.

Between you and me, I'm the quiet type. I like to keep to myself, and when I want to get away from it all, I do nothing. That's right. Once I stop swimming, I look like any other stick on the ocean floor, and nobody can see me.

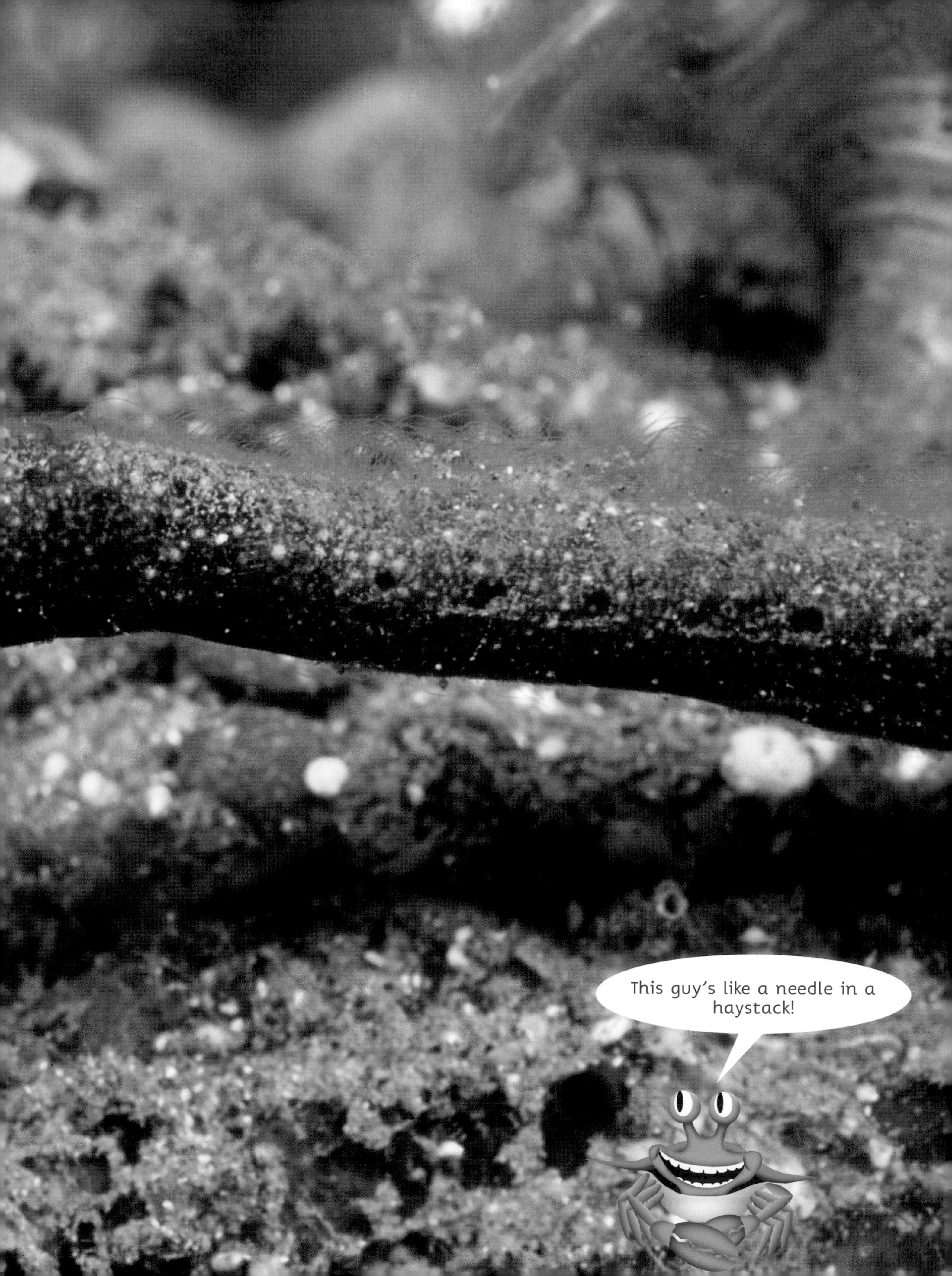
This guy's like a needle in a haystack!

HMMM...

THE STICK PIPEFISH IS A CLEVER FELLA.

The way he looks is a perfect example of how fish use camouflage, or the ability to blend in with their surroundings, to survive in this dog-eat-dog, I mean, fish-eat-fish world.

I don't look like a twig but came up with my own way to hide, which earned me the name Sand Diver.

With a name like that, what do you think I do all day?

Dive into the loose sand of course!

Once covered, I peep around to see what's going on.

And believe me, there's always something happening...

The Sand Diver can dive into the sand; after all, he has a hard head. If I tried to do that, I'd end up with a big headache!

I'm a Coral Goby, a tiny, timid fish, who also has a few tricks up his sleeve — wink, wink, nudge, nudge.

I'm transparent. That means you can see right through me.

When you look at me, remember I'm not green. Green is only the color of the coral I'm resting on today. Tomorrow I could be red, blue or orange, depending on where I'm taking my siesta.

Our lives are all about adaptation — using physical characteristics (the way you look) and some brains — to make it.

And what makes the sea so special is that everyone in it adapts in his or her own, unique way.

THE SKY'S NOT the ONLY PLACE WiTH CLOUDS.

We're silver fish called Scads, and we live in big schools, or "clouds," because we like each other a whole bunch and...

There's safety in numbers. Haven't you heard that before? Who's better at looking out for danger, one fish with two eyes or 1,000 fish with 2,000 eyes?

WHEN you're iN a big group, FRieNdS aNd FAMiLy offer protection, so stick close together.

It works for them, and it should work for you, too.

PSSSt!!! DOWN Here in the Sand!

I'm whispering because I don't want anybody to find me.

No, I'm not afraid of big fish. Actually, I'm the reason small fish are so careful.

I'm a Flatfish, a hunter that lurks in sandy areas. I'm as flat as a pancake and live buried, waiting for my yummy victims to swim by.

Once they do, My Sharp teeth and big, crooked Mouth go to Work.

Wow!
This is really
a fish-eat-fish
world!

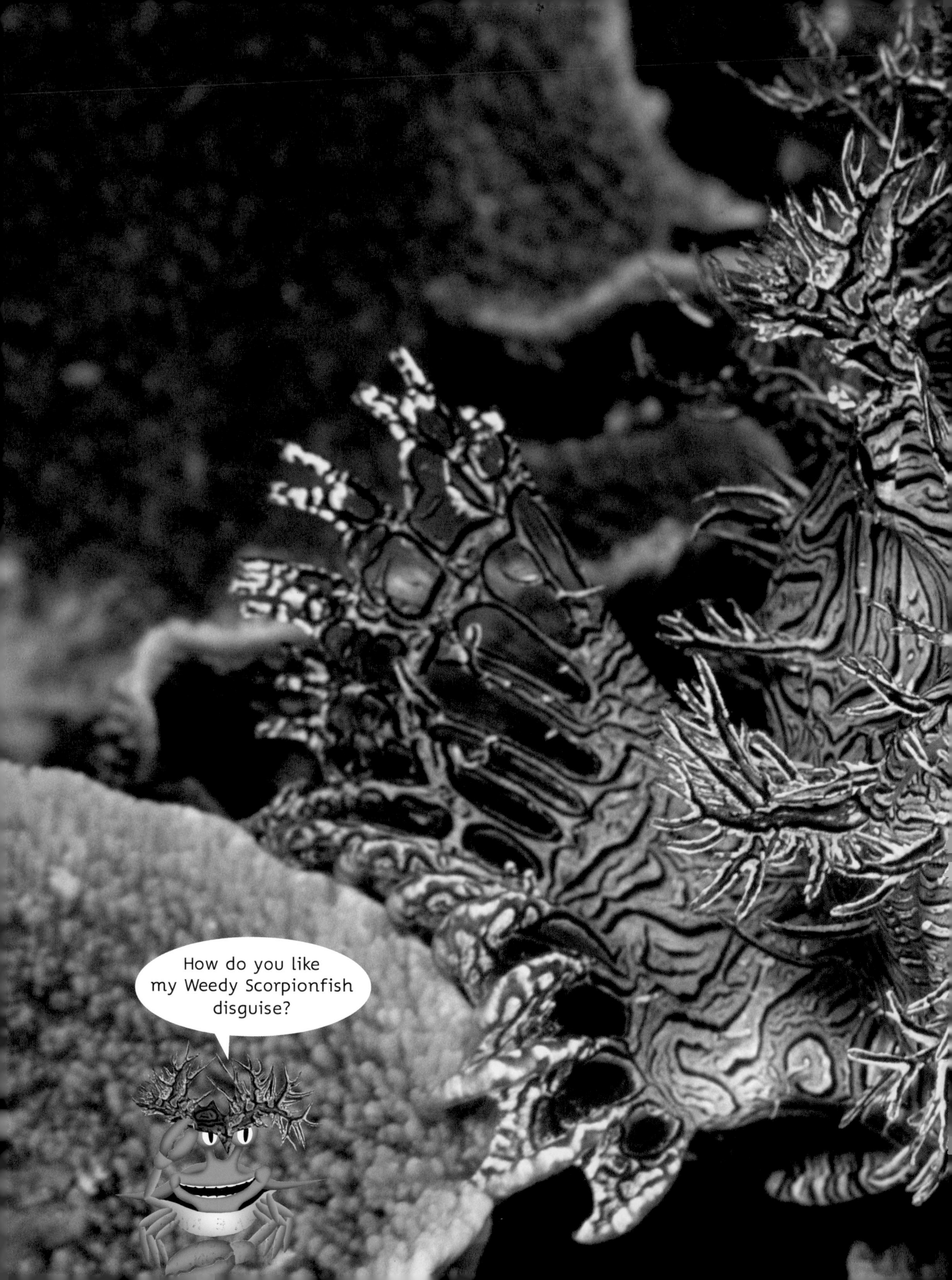
How do you like my Weedy Scorpionfish disguise?

YOU KNOW, I HAVE to HAND it to tHe FLatFiSH.

Can you imagine sitting buried in the sand all the time? By the end of the day, he's stiff as a board!

Like him, I'm not a good swimmer, so I also have to wait for lunch to get close enough so I can snatch it.

But I've created my own hunting technique. Instead of burying myself, I pretend I'm a clump of weeds.

No WoNder I'M caLLed a Weedy ScorpioNFiSH!

RETA E. KING LIBRARY
CHADRON STATE COLLEGE
CHADRON, NE 69337

I'M a FrogFiSH,
aNd LiKe tHe FLatFiSH
aNd Weedy ScorPioNFiSH,
I'M a MeMber oF tHe
Terrible SWiMMerS CLub.

If you look carefully, you can see why. I really don't have any fins or tail to speak of.

I would go hungry if I had to swim for a living. Therefore, I hang around for supper — home delivery style.

The bottom line is: I'm more rock than fish. I'm another great pretender, and do such a good job that tasty snacks seem to just come my way.

Mosaic Moray

Watch Your Fingers!

We may look like snakes, but we're fish, Moray Eels to be exact.

Unlike the Terrible Swimmers Club, we chase fish through the coral. Beware! You can run but you can't hide! Ha! Ha! Ha!

I'm History!

Yellow Moray

I'M AN OCTOPUS,

and it's safe to say everyone you've met with Charlie is jealous of me.

You really can't blame them. Let me tell you why:

I can change colors.

I can change the shape of my body.

I can grab lots of things with my eight arms.

Last, but not least, I can outsmart __most__ of the troops.

Okay. Super Octopus, you got me. I'm jealous, too.

He can't outsmart us!
COMMON DOLPHINS are
among the brightest
animals living in the sea.

Our intelligence is demonstrated by the way we talk to each other, hunt and protect ourselves.

We may look like fish, but we're mammals.

Mammals are warm-blooded animals that feed their young milk.

Hey, you're a mammal, too.

I don't buy all this talk about intelligence, camouflage and hide-and-seek games.

Because I'm a Nurse Shark, and sharks are the fastest and fiercest fish around. We're like the lions and tigers of the ocean, keeping it clean by feeding on the sick and the old.

We've been doing an excellent job for millions of years.

But recently something's come up...

ALTHOUGH WE DON'T LIKE to admit it, Caribbean Reef Sharks Like US and many other shark species are under attack...by MAN.

Can you believe millions of sharks are killed every year?

All this fishing is messing up Nature's delicate balance. Without us, the ocean wouldn't be healthy. And to top it off, a certain "electricity" and excitement would be gone forever.

But it doesn't have to be that way. Help us out! The solution is simple. Don't catch or eat sharks, and when you go to a restaurant, don't have any shark fin soup — gross!

Please!

NOW that the Sharks

I'm a baby Loggerhead Turtle, and unfort

Hear u

Have spoken, it's my turn.

ately, sea turtles are also having problems.

out...

Let's see what's going on.

THiS iS tHE DeaL.

We're at risk for a number of reasons:

We eat many things — sponges, lobster, even jellyfish.

I'm the mighty Leatherback, the world's largest turtle, and I love those jellyfish, but my juicy "jellies" look a lot like plastic bags litterbugs throw in the water.

And guess what happens?

Leatherbacks eat the bags, get really sick and die.

We also get caught in fishing line and hooks. When we get caught, we're underwater, and because we breathe air — like you — we drown.

A bunch of remoras are hitching a ride on the Leatherback. These fish use a suction disk near their heads to latch onto. In ancient times, people thought remoras slowed down ships, but even with this load, the powerful turtle swims with amazing speed. How many remoras can you count?

IN certain countries, people would enjoy a Hawksbill Turtle like me for dinner!

They would also jump at the chance to turn my beautiful shell into jewelry, or steal my eggs when I come ashore to nest!

So spread the word.

Don't be a litterbug!

Don't buy turtle products!

Don't disturb turtle nests!

I'M Sorry, but I Have to give you More bad NeWS...

I'm a Florida Manatee, and we're at risk of dying off, or going extinct. Since extinction is forever — and that's a very long time — we're fighting for survival.

It's not that people don't care about us. They do. The problem is we're really slow swimmers and quite often get hit by boats. Remember the Terrible Swimmers Club? Well, we got it started way back when.

SLOW

Hey boaters! Slow down!

Mr. Manatee, Cheer Up!

Where there's life, there's hope!

We, Nudibranches, were chatting about how there's so much to be thankful for. Crawling around the reef, we get to see all the beauty around us. And we're part of it, so keep the faith!

By the way, you could use some swimming lessons. Why don't you get in touch with those Common Dolphins? They're the best in the business.

Excellent idea!

THE "SILENT" WORLD

FROM THE SHALLOWS TO THE ABYS*
SO WHEN YOU HEAR NATTERING
DON'T b

Like you, we talk about everything.
Grunts like us can spend hours
yapping away. In our opinion,
there's no better way to spend a
sunny afternoon.

anything but Silent!
he ocean is Filled With voices,
ludibranches or gossiping Grunts,
Surprised!

You're about
to meet Bigmouth.

Blah. Blah. Blah.

I'm a big old Scorpionfish, and I've heard it all.

Day in and day out, my neighbors swim past my favorite ledge babbling away.

They forget I'm here, like a fly on the wall, looking and listening.

Here's the Latest...

This guy knows everybody's business.

RETA E. KING LIBRARY
CHADRON STATE COLLEGE
CHADRON, NE 69337

The Spider Crabs can't seem to stop Fighting...

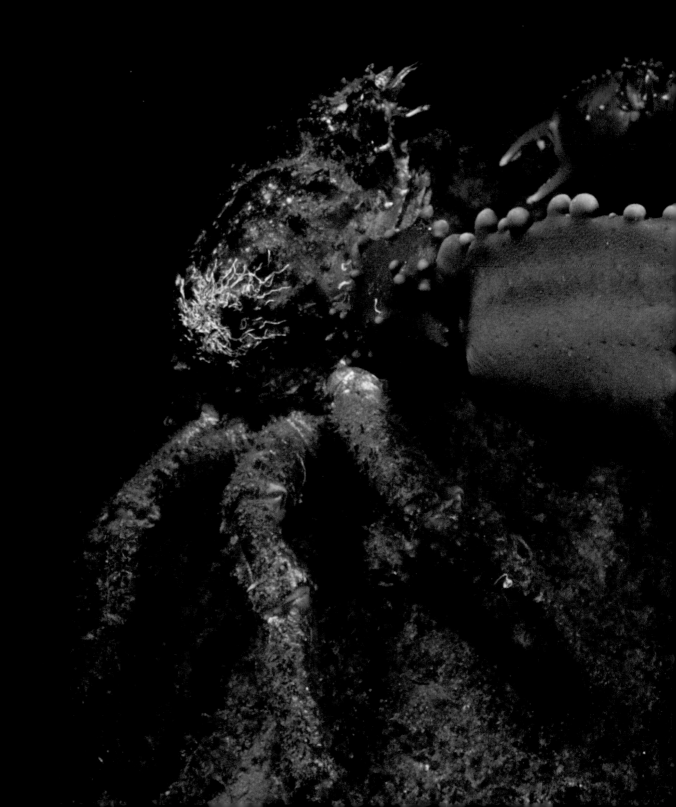

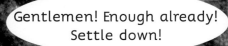

And the Red Pigfish is always looking for a party.

Let us know if you find one!

When you think about it, what goes on here is not much different than what goes on up there on dry land.

We're all tied into this wonderful web of life. The whole cast of characters — from the sharks, dolphins and turtles, to the folks who look like rocks, sticks, weeds or even spaghetti — depends on a clean and healthy ocean to survive. I guess you could say we're all in the same boat, or submarine, together.

And we're counting on your help. By saving the oceans, you're really saving the world. The Earth isn't called the "blue planet" for nothing, right? Most of it is covered by water!

As you found out, several of my friends are in deep trouble, but there's hope. Believe me, we can make a difference, but we're not going to do it overnight.

We're going to do it little by little, step by step. You and me.

What are we waiting for?